The FANTASY Soccer Wall

By Ann Bryant

Illustrated by Kelly Kennedy

Crabtree Publishing

www.crabtreebook

Crabtree Publishing Company
www.crabtreebooks.com
1-800-387-7650

616 Welland Ave.
St. Catharines, ON
L2M 5V6

PMB 59051, 350 Fifth Ave.
59th Floor,
New York, NY 10118

Published by Crabtree Publishing Company in 2016

First published in 2014 by Franklin Watts
(A division of Hachette Children's Books)

Text © Ann Bryant 2014
Illustration © Kelly Kennedy 2014

Series editor: Melanie Palmer
Series advisor: Catherine Glavina
Series designer: Cathryn Gilbert
Editor: Kathy Middleton
**Proofreader and
 notes to adults:** Shannon Welbourn
**Production coordinator and
 Prepress technician:** Ken Wright
Print coordinator: Amy Salter

Printed in Printed in the USA/082015/SN20150529

**Library and Archives Canada
Cataloguing in Publication**

Bryant, Ann, author
    The fantasy soccer wall / Ann Bryant ; Kelly
Kennedy, illustrator.

(Race further with reading)
Issued in print and electronic formats.
ISBN 978-0-7787-2061-4 (bound).--
ISBN 978-0-7787-2109-3 (pbk.).--
ISBN 978-1-4271-1667-3 (pdf).--
ISBN 978-1-4271-1659-8 (html)

    I. Kennedy, Kelly (Illustrator), illustrator
II. Title.

PZ7.B873Fa 2015   j823'.92   C2015-903056-0
                                   C2015-903057-9

**Library of Congress
Cataloging-in-Publication Data**

CIP available at Library of Congress

CHAPTER 1
The Game

Harry got changed in a flash for the big soccer game.

"Do you think we'll win, Mr. Gates?" he asked his teacher.

A boy named Brad answered him first.

"No, Yardley Elementary has better players than Berry Elementary."

Harry went red. He knew he wasn't as good at soccer as Brad.

"Just do your best. That's what matters," said Mr. Gates. "Come on, everyone," he added. "Time to warm up!"

Off they jogged to the soccer field chanting, "Berry School is the best!"
No one chanted louder than Harry.
He really wanted his team to win.

By half time, the score was one-nothing
for Yardley.

"Keep it up, everyone. We've still got
a good chance," said Mr. Gates.

In the second half, Harry tried harder
than ever. As soon as he spotted Brad in
a great position to score, he kicked the
ball perfectly to Brad's feet.

A second later, there was an enormous cheer as the ball shot straight from the tip of Brad's foot into the back of the net. "Goal! Yessss!"

It was a thrilling moment. Harry was hoping Brad might high five him for helping make the goal. But he didn't.

For the next twenty minutes the ball flew up and down the field. Then a moment came when one of the Yardley players was about to score. Harry ran like the wind determined to stop that goal. He got to the ball just in time to kick it out of the way. "Way to go, Harry!" cried Mr. Gates.

But a huge groan from the whole Berry team followed. Harry's kick had sent the ball off the field.

"Corner kick for Yardley," called Mr. Gates.

"What did you do that for?" Brad hissed at Harry.

Harry didn't even have time to answer before a loud cheer went up. The Yardley team had scored from the corner kick. Then the whistle blew, and the match was over. Once again, Yardley Elementary had won.

"Great effort, everyone!" said Mr. Gates,

as the team went back to the changeroom.

"You couldn't have played better."

"Except for Harry," muttered Brad. "It was

his fault we lost."

Mr. Gates didn't hear that. But Harry did,

and his spirits sank down to his shoes.

CHAPTER 2
No Ordinary Wall

It was break time and Harry was playing soccer in the playground. But he wasn't concentrating. He was looking over at a very steep hill on the other side of the playground. It was called "the mound," and no one was allowed near it. Harry liked to pretend that a monster lived inside it.

He snapped out of his daydream to find the ball flying toward him.

"Get it, Harry!" called Brad. "You're the closest!" Harry ran after the ball as it rolled onto the playground. Then he kicked it by mistake. By the time he caught up with it, he was right beside the mound.

"Harry Bing!" called Mrs. Carter, the lunch lady, sternly. "Get away from the mound this instant! You know it is forbidden to play there. Now go and stand by the wall for three minutes!"

Children had to stand by the wall if they broke the rules. Harry trudged off to stand by the wall for three minutes.

He was sure Brad had kicked the ball hard on purpose to get him into trouble. Ever since the match against Yardley, Brad had been mean to him.

He sighed and stared at the wall. Maybe if he invented a game it would make the three minutes go faster.

Yes! He could pretend the wall was a massive computer with superpowers.

He would control the computer, and every brick in the wall was someone in the school. "Okay, this one is Brad Bates," he whispered, touching the brick right in front of his nose. "Make him fall over."

At that very moment, a screech filled
the air. Harry looked over at the soccer
game. Brad was on the ground. He got up
a moment later with a scowl on his face
and said, "Someone tripped me."

Harry's eyes flew open and his heart
beat faster. Did the wall really have
superpowers?

No, that was impossible. All the same,
he would try it again. Tapping the brick
that glowed, he said, "Make Mrs. Carter
blow her whistle."

Harry had hardly finished speaking
when Mrs. Carter blew her whistle.
Everyone immediately stood still.
"Time to line up!" she announced.

But Harry didn't want to line up. He wanted to stay at the wall. It was totally amazing. The wall really did have superpowers.

He quickly tapped the glowing brick again. "Make Mrs. Lee forget all about that test she was going to give us this afternoon."

CHAPTER 3
A Strange Discovery

Mrs. Lee stood at the front of the class.

"Now, I know I said I was going to give you a test," she began as soon as everyone was quiet, "but the photocopier is broken."

Harry sat on the edge of his chair.

"So you are lucky," went on Mrs. Lee.

"No test today!"

Everybody cheered, but Harry stayed silent. He was thinking about the wall. It absolutely must have superpowers! He couldn't wait for school to finish so he could try it out again.

When the bell rang, Harry got ready very slowly. Then he went to the library and spent a very long time choosing a book. Finally, when everyone else had gone home, he slipped into the empty playground and hurried over to the wall. His heart was pounding with excitement. This was going to be great.

"Alright," he said out loud, "I think I'll start with the school cook." Harry reached up and tapped the glowing brick.

"Make Mrs. Blanch put chocolate pudding on the menu every day this term!"

Suddenly, there was a noise like a growl from behind the wall. He gasped. The growling grew louder. Maybe a monster really did live in the mound! It was just behind the wall. Harry's heart thumped as a wisp of smoke curled out of the top.

Was the monster a dragon? He nearly jumped out of his skin at the sound of footsteps right behind him.

"Who were you talking to?"

It was a shock to see Brad standing there.

"No one."

"Yes you were. And you were tapping the wall. I saw you," accused Brad.

Harry was so filled with fear he could hardly speak. "There's a dragon...," was all he managed to utter.

"That's a bulldozer you hear. It's on the other side of the wall," said Brad, sneering. "They're flattening the mound to make more playground. Didn't you even know that?"

"But what about…the dragon?"

"Don't be stupid!" said Brad.

"There's no such thing as a dragon."

He turned to walk away, but turned back almost immediately as a sharp shriek filled the air. Then both boys stared in horror as the top of the mound erupted to reveal an angry, green and silver dragon.

CHAPTER 4
Stop the Bulldozer!

The dragon spread its spiky leather wings and arched its neck. With one leap, it launched itself into the playground, its gleaming eyes fixed on Harry and Brad.

Then with a shuddering breath, it suddenly stopped next to the mound.

Brad trembled and grabbed onto Harry. "Quick!" he whispered urgently. "It's falling asleep! Let's go before it wakes up."

Brad had only moved a few steps when they both heard an angry roar. The dragon had woken and reared up, nostrils flaring. Brad shot straight back to Harry's side and stood there, shaking. Then, letting out a long snort, the dragon flopped down once again.

"We're trapped," whispered Brad.

"Maybe not," said Harry, a thoughtful look on his face.

"What do you mean?" asked Brad, grabbing Harry's arm.

"The wall has superpowers," said Harry.

"We just need to find the glowing brick."

Brad looked as though he was about to sneer again, but then changed his mind. "So m-m-make the bulldozer g-g-get to work!" he stammered. As the words were leaving his mouth, something incredible happened. Two tiny dragons slowly clambered out of the mound.

One of them tumbled down the side
and rolled over the sleeping dragon.
The other one fell back inside.

"The mother dragon is protecting her
babies," breathed Harry. "She thought
we were going to hurt them."

And at that very moment, a gravelly, grating roar filled the air. The bulldozers were at work, and the mother dragon hadn't even stirred from her deep sleep. "We've got to warn her!" said Harry. "The baby dragon in the mound will get completely crushed."

Brad seemed frozen to the spot.

"W-w-what can we do?"

"Stop the bulldozers," said Harry.

"But how?" asked Brad, his teeth chattering with fear.

"Tap every single brick in the wall," said Harry firmly, "until we find the right one. With each tap, say the words: Make the bulldozers stop!"

Brad's face was pale with fear.

"Go!" said Harry.

The boys worked and worked, jumping for the high bricks, reaching for the faraway bricks, bending for the low ones. Together they tapped and tapped until suddenly the noise of the bulldozers stopped.

"We did it!" cried Brad.

Harry gulped. "We still have to warn the mother dragon," he said.

"No way," said Brad, wide-eyed.

Harry didn't reply. Taking a deep breath,
he crept toward the dragon on shaky legs.

He had never felt more scared in his life as he
reached out and touched her wrinkled neck.

Instantly she raised her head. Harry pointed

to the baby dragon next to her. The dragon's

eyes flashed, and she picked it up in her

mouth. Then with a flick of her tail she

scooped the other baby out of the mound. A

moment later she had taken off into the sky.

Harry and Brad were glued to the spot. They watched in amazement as the dragon rose over the playground with her babies. Over the woods she soared. Up and away she flew until she was no more than a tiny dot in the distance.

CHAPTER 5
The Rematch

The next day Harry got to school early.
He went to the playground to find Brad
waiting for him. Brad still looked wide-eyed.
"Did it really happen, Harry?" he asked.
Harry nodded. "I think so. Let's test it again."
He found the glowing brick and tapped it.
"Make us beat Yardley this afternoon."

The Berry vs Yardley match was the most exciting game ever. With less than a minute to go, the score was one-nothing for Berry. But the Yardley team had the ball.

"Go, Harry!" screamed Brad, as a Yardley player booted the ball toward the goal.

It was happening exactly as it had in the last game. Harry ran his hardest, managing to kick the ball out of the way just in time.

But this time Brad was in position. He stopped the ball from going off the field and dribbled it away from Yardley's players.

The final whistle blew.

"Great teamwork!" yelled Mr. Gates.

The game was over. Berry had won.

Harry and Brad went to pick up their hoodies from behind the net. But something caught their eye first—a tiny, hard, green egg, covered in silver swirls.

"Wow!" gasped Brad.

"Let's take it to the woods," whispered Harry. "It'll be safe there."

So, when no one was looking, they slipped away and gently placed the egg in a hollow tree trunk.

Jogging back onto the field they heard a swishing sound from high above and they both looked up. Two bright eyes glinted down at them from the blue sky. Then one of them closed and opened again. A moment later the sky clouded over.

"Come on, you two heroes!" Mr. Gates called from the other end of the field. "You did an outstanding job today!" Brad grinned at Harry. Harry grinned back. And the two of them high fived each other. "Yes, we did!"

Notes for Adults

Race Further with Reading is the next entertaining level up for young readers from *Race Ahead with Reading*. Longer, more in-depth chapters and fun illustrations help children build up their vocabulary and reading skills in a fun way.

THE FOLLOWING BEFORE, DURING, AND AFTER READING ACTIVITY SUGGESTIONS SUPPORT LITERACY SKILL DEVELOPMENT AND CAN ENRICH SHARED READING EXPERIENCES:

BEFORE

1. Make reading fun! Choose a time to read when you and the reader are relaxed and have time to share the story together. Don't forget to give praise! Children learn best in a positive environment.
2. Before reading, ask the reader to look at the title and illustrations on the cover of the book **The Fantasy Soccer Wall**. Invite them to make predictions about what will happen in the story. They may make use of prior knowledge and make connections to other stories they have heard or read about a similar character.

DURING

3. Encourage readers to determine unfamiliar words themselves by using clues from the text and illustrations.
4. During reading, encourage the child to review his or her understanding and see if they want to revise their predictions midway. Encourage the reader to make text-to-text connections, choosing a part of the story that reminds them of another story they have read; and text-to-self connections, choosing a part of the story that relates to their own personal experiences; and text-to-world connections, choosing a part of the story that reminds them of something that happened in the real world.

AFTER

5. Ask the reader who the main characters are. Describe how the characters' traits or feelings impact the story.
6. Have the child retell the story in their own words. Ask him or her to think about the predictions they made before reading the story. How were they the same or different?

7. Encourage the reader to refer to parts in the story by the chapters the events occurred in and explain how the story developed.

DISCUSSION QUESTIONS FOR KIDS

8. From your point of view, how did you think the relationship between Harry and Brad would progress by the end of the story? Use evidence from the story to explain your point.
9. Choose one of the illustrations from the story. How do the details in the picture help you understand a part of the story better? Or, what do the illustrations tell you that is not in the text?
10. What part of the story surprised you? Why was it a surprise?
11. How did Brad's character change throughout this story, and how did Harry respond to these changes?
12. What moral, or lesson, can you take from this story?
13. Create your own story or drawing about something you felt was magical, or a time you wish you had superpowers.
14. Have you read another story by the same author? Compare the stories you have read by the same author or compare this story to other books in the **Race Further with Reading** series.
15. Have you ever been on a team? Describe what you think is important for being a part of a team and compare this to the characters in the story. (ie. Harry, Brad, Mr. Gates)